'Attila stuck her head through the top of her cage and called for silence.

"Sisters! Listen to me for I have much to say." They listened. "The old hen and I have a plan for all of us to escape from this flea-infested rat-hole."

At this the hens cheered madly. "Hooray! Hooray!"

She went on to explain the plan which seemed both simple and possible. Then the old hen spoke. She told them about Attila's dream. She told the story so well that the hens shivered with dread at her pictures of the soup monster. They saw the grassy meadow, and felt the fresh breeze from the land of grain and greenness.

"The journey will not be easy. Many of you won't make it to the end. Will you come with us?"

"We will come! We will come!" cheered the hens. "Hooray for Attila and the old hen!"'

Attila is too big and stroppy a hen to settle for life on a dirty, smelly battery farm – and she certainly has no intention of ending up as chicken soup. She hatches a plan for the greatest *egg*scape in the whole history of henery . . .

Attila the Hen, a hilarious and exciting adventure, is Paddy Mounter's first children's book to be published by Yearling Books.

ATTILA THE HEN

Attila the Hen
PADDY MOUNTER

YEARLING BOOKS

ATTILA THE HEN
A YEARLING BOOK 0 440 86264 7

First published in Great Britain by Doubleday, a division of
Transworld Publishers Ltd.

PRINTING HISTORY
Doubleday edition published 1989
Yearling edition published 1991
Yearling edition reprinted 1991 (twice)

This book is set in 14/16pt Century Schoolbook by
Chippendale Type Limited, Otley, West Yorkshire.

Yearling Books are published by Transworld Publishers Ltd.,
61–63 Uxbridge Road, Ealing, London W5 5SA, in Australia by
Transworld Publishers (Australia) Pty. Ltd., 15–23 Helles
Avenue, Moorebank, NSW 2170, and in New Zealand by
Transworld Publishers (N.Z.) Ltd., Cnr. Moselle and Waipareira
Avenues, Henderson, Auckland.

Printed and bound in Great Britain by
Cox & Wyman Ltd., Reading, Berks.

To Patsy, Alice, Emily, Jack
and the dog.

ATTILA THE EGG

The next time you have a boiled egg for breakfast, take a good look at it. It will almost certainly be a proper egg-shaped egg that fits nicely in your egg-cup. Is this because the clever hens always lay eggs of just the right size and shape? No, it's not. If you could take a look at the millions of eggs that are laid every day, you'd find that some would be very big, with two or even three yolks inside. Some would be very small, maybe no bigger than a pigeon's egg. If you were really lucky you might come across an egg that had two shells, one inside the other like a Russian doll. Once in a bright blue moon you might find an egg shaped like a banana.

Now the reason that you can't buy these interesting eggs for your breakfast, is that they are sorted – taken away and used for something else. Only egg-shaped eggs are wanted for the shops, or allowed to hatch into hen-shaped hens.

Late in the afternoon of Monday 1st April, in a large concrete shed, on the edge of a great city, the biggest hen's egg in the world was moving slowly along a conveyor belt. It was by far the biggest of all the thousands of eggs that surrounded it and it was about to be sorted. The two girls who did this job had had a long, boring day. Alice had been to a party the night before and she was trying not to yawn. Emily thought she was catching a cold and she was trying not to sneeze.

'I think I'm catching a . . . aaachooo!' said Emily, and

missed sorting the biggest egg in the world.

Alice looked at her. 'Sorry, Em, I was miles away. What did you sayyyyyawn . . . ? Oh dear!' As she yawned, the biggest egg in the world went by on its way to the hatching shed.

So Attila the Egg escaped the sorting to be hatched into this story, which is as it should be because there's not much future for a story called *Attila the Omelette*.

THE PLOT IS HATCHED

The hatching shed was a quiet, peaceful place. Attila the Egg was one of thousands lying in huge trays, stacked one above the other in long rows. The idea of a hatchery is quite simple. The eggs are tricked into thinking that they are being sat on by a hen. They are kept in a warm, dark place and turned over every few hours. After a while a miracle happens and the eggs hatch into chicks.

Eric was seventeen years old. Although he quite liked his job at the hatchery, checking eggs all day wasn't really his idea of fun.

He had been stacking a new batch of eggs into the hatching trays when he came across the biggest egg in the world. It was unbelievable. He picked it up.

'Wow! What an egg!'

Eric had found one or two out-of-the-ordinary eggs before and had thrown them in the bin without a thought. This was different.

'I bet the girls on the sorting line let it through as a joke,' he said. For a moment he weighed the big egg in his hand. It felt warm and alive.

'Well, just for a joke I'm going to keep it,' decided Eric. Gently he put the egg back in the tray. 'From now on, big egg, your old pal Eric's going to be your mum.'

Every day for the next three weeks Eric chatted to his pet egg.

'Good morning, egg,' he would say, or 'How're you doing, egg?' He smiled at himself. 'I must be going daft. I'll be clucking at it soon.'

And so it was that in the middle of a

Sunday night, faint pecking sounds could be heard coming from the eggs. Soon beaks and little wobbly heads appeared through the shells. In a few hours the silent trays of eggs had hatched into a mass of hopping, chirping chicks.

14

POP!!

TICK!

There were a few eggs that hadn't hatched and one of these was the giant egg. It lay still and silent, like a brown rock in a fluffy yellow sea. The chicks ignored it. Suddenly – without any warning – the giant egg stood on its end. Chicks scrambled over each other to get away and stood staring at it in a frightened circle. The huge egg began to quiver. A long rattle of pecks, like a machine gun, came from inside. Then came louder pecks, more like a road drill, a strangled squeak and a long silence. The chicks jumped back! The egg had started to bounce, little hops at first but getting bigger and bigger. Then it was off, bouncing across the tray, scattering chicks and ticking like a time bomb. Round and round, higher and higher it went, until it hit the tray above and exploded with a pop and a screech.

15

Something very
odd and very
cross lay on
its back in the
middle of the

tray. Attila the chick had just got
herself hatched and it put her in a
bad mood that was to last the rest of
her life.

Eric was smiling when he arrived
for work that morning. The first
thing he did was to check his pet egg.

'Well, big egg, this is it,' he said,
peeping into the tray. 'Let's see what
you've hatched yourself into.'

Eric stopped smiling. A tall 'thing'
with a murderous look in its eye
glared at him over the heads of the
other chicks. For a long time they
stared at each other – then Eric
began to laugh. He leant against the
nearest wall and laughed until his
sides ached and tears ran down his
cheeks.

'What a monster!' he gasped. 'You
have got to be "Attila the Hen",' and

he laughed so much at his own joke that he had to sit down on the floor.

The chick was so odd-looking that even a short-sighted mother hen would have found it hard to be proud of her. The only fluff she had was on top of her head, where it was long and thick and stuck out like a lavatory brush. Her large beak had been bent trying to escape from the egg, so that with her long legs she looked like a bad-tempered old boxer, standing on stilts, wearing his granny's yellow hat. Eric stood up and wiped his eyes. He looked at his pet and sighed. 'It seems a pity but I suppose I'd better give you the chop.' He bent over the tray to pick her up. She pecked him – hard.

'Ouch! Oh, what the heck. Have it your own way, Attila. Stay where you are and good luck – you'll need it.'

She pecked him again later when he was bundling her and the other chicks into cardboard boxes marked: DAY-OLD CHICKS – HANDLE WITH CARE.

For what seemed like hours, the chicks bounced around in the stuffy boxes while they were roughly loaded and unloaded, like parcels at the post office. Then suddenly the boxes were torn open and the chicks tumbled out into their new home.

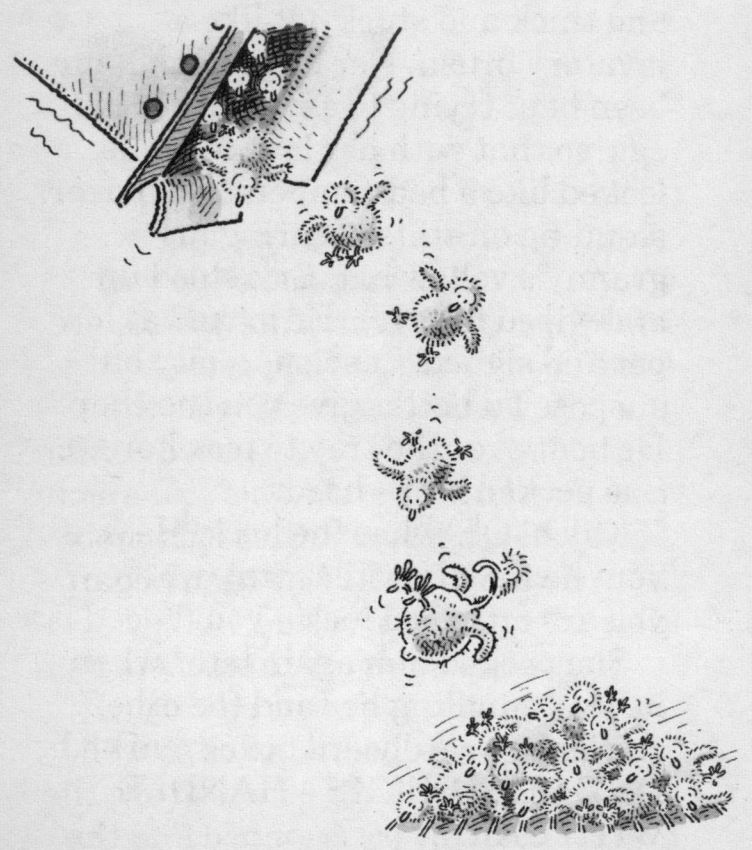

ATTILA THE CHICK

At first, life in the rearing shed was great. All the chicks had to do was eat and grow bigger. Young hens are very good at this so they grew quickly, feathers sprouting as the fluff disappeared. This pleased Attila because, although she was still much bigger, feathers made her look more like the other birds. She then began to look on the bright side.

'If this is a hen's life then it's not so bad,' she said. 'We must be very important to be looked after so well.'

It didn't last. As the hens grew, the cages became very cramped and the squabbling started. Hens have a very simple way of living together. Big hens peck smaller hens, who peck smaller hens, and so on down the pecking order to the smallest hen, who is pecked by everyone.

Duster was the exception to this rule. She was a stroppy little hen who looked as if she'd been used to clean the cobwebs off the ceiling. She was the only one that wasn't afraid of Attila.

'Just my luck to get stuck in the same cage as that feathered freak,' she grumbled. 'Move over, Buster, I'm squashed to bits.'

Buster was a large, good-natured hen who quite enjoyed Duster's grumbles. She shuffled her feet and pretended to move over.

The young hens' troubles really began with a noise like a singing pig dancing on bagpipes.

'SQUARRRRRK! SCREEEEECH!' SQUARRRRRK!'

SQUAAWK!! **SCREEECH!! SQUAAWK!**

They were dozing at the end of a long, boring day.

'What's that horrible noise?' said Attila.

'Dunno! Perhaps someone's being murdered,' said Duster hopefully. 'Sounds like that daft Paxo two cages down.'

It was Paxo. She wasn't being murdered, she had laid an egg. It wasn't a big egg but Paxo, a rather noisy hen, was very proud of it.

At last the hens had something to talk about.

'Speaking for myself, I think she's making a lot of fuss about nothing.'

'Yes, after all it is a very small egg.'

'True. I must say I would prefer a darker shade of brown.'

Secretly they couldn't wait to lay eggs of their own. Only Duster was uneasy about the arrival of an egg.

'Eggs are trouble. It's a bad omen and no good will come of it.'

'Nonsense,' said Buster, 'what harm could there be in one nice little egg?'

Before dawn the next day, the shed door banged open. The lights came on and a gang of men poured into the rearing shed. They threw open the cage doors and began grabbing the terrified hens by the legs. For the men, it was just another morning's work. They chatted and joked as they carried handfuls of squeaking, flapping birds out of the shed and stuffed them into wire crates on the back of an open lorry. For the hens, the easy life was over.

The journey that followed gave the young hens their first taste of the outside world. Rain drifted down through a grey and miserable morning. They were squashed in crates, as stiff and cold as sardines in a tin. Although Attila was frozen to her feather-roots she took notice of the country they were travelling through. The rush and noise of the towns was frightening but the first sight of green countryside filled her with a longing she didn't understand. Gradually the hedges and trees disappeared as the lorry crawled its way up on to a high and empty plain.

Later she must have fallen asleep, because it was almost dark when her crate was dragged from the lorry. Attila woke up at Sunnycluck Farm, Home of Happy Hens, Producers of Farm-Fresh Eggs.

DOWN ON SUNNYCLUCK FARM

Sunnycluck Farm was a mess. It was run by farmer William Limpditch, known as 'Battery Bill'. Like most farmers, Bill never threw anything away. He kept all his old cars and farm machinery and let them rust away instead. He mended everything with a piece of wire and a hammer, and the holes in the few hedges that he hadn't ploughed up were stopped with old bedsteads.

Battery Bill lived with his wife Eva, and two lumpy sons, Wayne and Abel, in a grey concrete house. It stood in a grey concrete yard, surrounded by grey concrete farm buildings.

The battery shed wasn't concrete; it was old, wooden and falling to bits, with a faded sign on one end that read: SUNNYCLUCK FARM, HOME OF HAPPY HENS. You could smell the farm a mile away.

Bill was not an unkind man. He'd kept hens all his life. He couldn't see anything wrong or cruel about it.

'Only happy hens lay eggs and that's that,' he said and as far as he was concerned, that was the end of the argument.

The new batch of young hens were not happy. When the first rays of the rising sun crept through the dusty windows, they saw what an awful place they'd been brought to. The

cages were filthy and covered in rust. They were stacked three high in long rows with four hens squeezed into every cage. It looked like a dark smelly supermarket that only sold hens. Attila was lucky, she was in a top cage, which meant that she could stretch her neck through the wire and peck at the cobwebs that hung from the roof. Duster and Buster had ended up in the same cage.

'Isn't it nice that we've all managed to stay together?' said Buster.

Duster glared at her. 'Yes, isn't it?' she snapped.

The fourth hen had been crouched in the corner of the cage when they arrived. Half her feathers were missing and she looked very old. Eventually her silence got on Attila's nerves.

'What's up with you?' she asked rudely. 'You look half dead!'

Slowly the old hen raised her head. She had a voice like a rusty hinge.

'By rights I should be all dead.
I should have been carted and
    cooked
and clamped in a can.
Boiled up for broth in a vat.
Bashed up and mashed up for pâté
    or Spam.
Or squashed in a tin for the cat.'

'She's off her head,' said Duster.
The old hen stood up and squinted
at the new arrivals. 'Just my little
joke about what is to be,' she
laughed. 'Listen, sisters, as this is the
first day of your new life, I will tell
you the short, sad story of the battery
hen. For the next year you will live a
cramped life of egg-laying misery.
You will squabble and fight and
become like me. If you are a good
layer you may be allowed to live a
little longer. But in the end, it's the
chicken-soup lorry for all of us, as
sure as eggs is eggs.'

Attila stared at her. 'But they can't
do that.'

'Why not?' said the old hen. 'What's to stop them?'

Attila had gone as red as a raspberry and her eyes stuck out like gobstoppers.

'Me!' she screamed. 'That's what!'

Just for a moment the old hen stared up at the huge bird with a faraway look in her eye. Then she shook her head and crawled back into the corner. 'As sure as eggs is eggs,' she whispered.

AS SURE AS EGGS IS EGGS

Gradually the old hen's words came true. One by one the young hens began to lay. Attila laid the first of many eggs.

It started as a funny feeling in the pit of her stomach, as if she'd swallowed a large marble. Soon it felt like a golf ball, then a potato. She flapped her wings, coughed, jumped up and down, sneezed, and there it was, a big brown egg. Attila didn't know whether to be pleased or not.

'Hey, look, I've laid an egg! I've laid an egg!' she squawked.

'Good for you!' said Buster.

'So what?' said Duster. 'By the noise you were making we thought you'd laid a brick.'

Attila managed to sit on it for a while, then it rolled under the wire where she couldn't reach it. After that she didn't bother, she just let her eggs roll away to be collected with all the others.

Time went by, spring changed to summer, and the noise and heat in the battery house became unbearable. The crowded hens had nothing to do but peck and squabble all through the long hot days. The old hen watched sadly from her corner. She'd seen it all before.

Peck! Peck! 'Shove over, fatso.'

'Do you want the whole cage to yourself?' Peck! Peck!

'Shut your beak, bird-brain, or you'll wish you'd never been hatched.' Peck! Peck! Peck!

Some of the smaller hens had lost most of their feathers. Even Attila had a bald patch here and there.

It was the night after a very hot and hopeless day that Attila had the dream. The lights went out as usual for the few hours of darkness the hens were allowed. Almost at once Attila fell into a deep sleep. She dreamt that she was running after a bright circle of light, but no matter how fast she ran, the light never seemed any nearer. Days or weeks flashed by in a jumble of dreams until the light stopped over a meadow and turned into the setting sun. The meadow sloped steeply down to a clear stream. White and yellow flowers speckled the grass – and trees, full of fruit, shaded a small wooden house. There were chicks and hens running in and out of the door, and scratching happily in the evening sunshine. More than anything Attila wanted to be there. She could feel the warm sun and the breeze on her feathers but she couldn't move, her feet seemed to have taken root in the soft earth.

The sun went behind a cloud, it grew very dark and the meadow disappeared. Now she was in a huge cage being pushed from behind by scratching, pecking hens towards something horrible in the darkness. A hot wind, like bad breath, cleared the smoke in front of her and Attila saw the chicken-soup monster. It was huge. Flames roared from its boiling jaws. The great steel body heaved with pistons and hissed with steam. It rumbled with grinding cogs and flying pulleys. High on its head, in a little glass box, sat the man who worked the long arms with the wire claws that grabbed fistfuls of scrawny hens, lifted them high into the steam and dropped them, screeching, into the horrible jaws. The monster crouched on a mountain of soup cans that winked and glittered in the light of the flames. A steady rain of cans fell from chutes high in the monster's sides.

Attila was forced towards the nightmare. Terrified hens crushed against her but there was no escape. The claw gathered them up into the reeking cloud. Then they were falling. There was a desperate flapping of tatty wings. Flames leapt up towards Attila. She screamed and the awful sound woke her and all the battery house.

The hens grumbled for a while and went back to sleep, but not Attila. For two days she crouched against the wire, staring into the haze beyond the dusty windows. The old hen talked gently to her but there was no answer. She seemed to be in a trance.

'I think she will die,' said the old hen. 'I've seen it happen many times before.'

So it came as quite a shock on the third night after the dream, when

Attila suddenly came to life with a squeak. Buster and Duster had taken to using her as a pillow. She shook them off like a couple of sparrows and stood up, feathers on end, looking huge in the darkness. Her eyes flashed and sparked like two Catherine wheels.

'We must get away or it will eat us all,' she screeched. 'I've felt its claws, I've smelt its horrible breath. We've got to get away!' She threw herself at the cage door like a mad thing. Again and again the big hen crashed against the wire while the whole line of cages rocked and shook. All down the row, hens screeched in alarm. CRASH! 'Help!' CRASH! 'It's an earthquake!' CRASH! 'We're all doomed!' THWANG!

Suddenly the door gave way. The cage was open. Attila sank back like a punctured balloon and stared at what she had done.

They all stared in disbelief.

'It is a miracle,' whispered the old hen. 'It is the sign I had given up all

hope of. We must close the door
again. Battery Bill mustn't know we
can open his cages.'

'Close it!' shrieked Duster. 'Not on
your nelly – I'm off.'

'Wait!' said the old hen, standing in
front of the open door. 'How far do
you think you will get, all alone in
the great outside?' Duster glared at
her but said nothing.

'Attila is right. We must get away,
but we must do it together. She has
shown us the way. Can't you see?

One big hen is no stronger than four hens added together. And four hens, take away one door, multiplied by one thousand equals four thousand. Therefore, four thousand hens times one fat farmer must add up to Battery Bill's number being up.' She stared at them triumphantly. 'It will be the greatest escape in the whole history of henery.'

After a long pause Buster said, 'Henry who?'

And Duster said, 'If there's one thing I hate more than riddles, it's sums.'

And Attila said, 'My head hurts.'

The old hen didn't care what they thought. From the moment Attila battered open their cage door, the dotty old bird was sure she'd been sent to save them. For the next few days she fussed around like a mother hen with one chick. Attila began to look on the older bird as a friend and told her about her dreams.

The old hen grew very excited. 'Your dreams are the shadows of our future. I have the gift to tell you what they mean.' She fixed Attila with her beady little eye.

'The dark dream tells us that if we do nothing, then like all our sisters before us, we'll be fed to the soup monster.' She shuddered at the thought. 'But the light in the dream tells us that if we break free and follow the sun westwards for many days, we will find happiness in a land flowing with grain and greenery. You, Attila the Hen, have been sent to lead us to freedom.'

PLANS ARE LAID

When the lights went out that third night after the dream, Attila stuck her head through the top of her cage and called for silence.

'Sisters! Listen to me for I have much to say.' They listened. A hen who could batter down doors was worth a hearing.

'The old hen and I have a plan for all of us to escape from this flea-infested rat-hole.'

At this the hens cheered madly. 'Hooray! Hooray!'

She went on to explain the plan which seemed both simple and possible. Then the old hen spoke. She told them about Attila's dream. She told the story so well that the hens shivered with dread at her pictures of the soup monster. They saw the grassy meadow, and felt the fresh breeze from the land of grain and greenness.

'The journey will not be easy. Many of you won't make it to the end. Will you come with us?'

'We will come! We will come!' cheered the hens. 'Hooray for Attila and the old hen!'

For the rest of the night the hens couldn't sleep. The cages buzzed and cackled with excitement. As soon as the lights came on they started to carry out the plan: press-ups, wing-flaps, and hopping-on-the-spot. In every cage, three hens could be seen cowering away from a fourth hen who was jumping and flapping like a demented yo-yo. When she'd finished, another hen took her place and did the same. They kept at it all day until the lights went out and they collapsed, exhausted, while the

dust and feathers settled around them.

'I feel awful but happy,' said Buster.

'You mean you feel awfully happy,' said Duster. Her friends looked at her and fell about laughing. Duster didn't often make jokes.

It was the same the next day and the next, from morning till night. Attila didn't have to bully them, the hens were so pleased to have something to do.

After a week, Battery Bill realized that things were not as they should be. His hens looked fit and well. They were eating more but laying fewer eggs. And the noise! What were they doing? He tried spying through the windows but couldn't see a thing for dust. Once he tried to catch them out by nipping quickly into the shed. Before he was halfway through the door the noise had stopped and all he found were thousands of beady eyes staring at him. What he also found was Wayne having a crafty cigarette behind the door. It was the only place he could be sure his father wouldn't smell the smoke.

'You sneaky little weasel!' shouted Bill and he clipped the boy round the ear. Wayne dropped the cigarette and wailed. Bill was hopping mad.

'As if those dratted hens weren't costing me enough without you wasting money on filthy fags.'

He helped his son through the door with his large welly boot and slammed it shut.

'And I've half a mind to phone the soup lorry to fetch you lot and all,' he shouted, looking round at the silent hens. After a while he calmed down. He picked up the half-smoked cigarette and finished it off.

And so it was that on a fine morning at the end of July, all that was laid by the hens of Sunnycluck Farm was one small, light brown egg (nothing could stop Paxo). Bill sat down to breakfast and stared at the boiled egg in front of him.

'I don't understand it. Four thousand of the healthiest hens in the country and one small egg.' He thumped the table with his fist. 'I won't have it!' Cups and cornflakes went everywhere.

'Never mind, dear,' said his wife. 'Hens will be hens.' – 'And farmers will be pigs,' she muttered to herself as she picked the bits off the floor.

Bill stood up. He picked up his stick, threw the egg at the dogs and stomped into the yard in his socks.

Wham! The shed door slammed against the wall. Bill stood in the middle of his battery house and ranted at his hens. 'I won't have it!' He beat the cages with his stick. 'I . . . will . . . not . . . have . . . it!' He swore at them and jumped up and down in his socks. 'After all I've done for you — given you nice warm cages, lots of

tasty fish-meal to eat, so you don't have to scratch in the dust for nasty slugs and worms and things. All you have to do is lay a few eggs, it's not much to ask, is it?'

He began to plead with them. They were ruining him, he said. If they didn't lay soon he would be bankrupt. Finally he got down on his knees in the muck and feathers. 'Just a few eggs . . . Please . . . '

Silence.

Then a hen called Edwina, in one of the lower cages, made a very rude remark in Chickenese about the size of Bill's bum. There were a couple of suppressed squeaks, then the whole battery house burst into hysterical cackling. Bill didn't understand the joke but he knew for certain they were laughing at him.

'Right!' he spluttered, jumping up. 'Right, that's it! You've asked for it!' and he stormed off to phone the soup lorry.

THE GREAT EGGSCAPE

The hens were ready. They'd heard the lorry arrive even before Bill and his family were up. Now they listened to the noises outside, like an army before a battle. Clanking crates, barking dogs and Bill, shouting at his sons and the men who'd come to help. Inside the shed all eyes were on the battery-house door.

It opened – in strode Bill and stood before them with his hands on his hips.

'Right, you lot, you had your chance. Now it's . . . ' He stopped. Something was wrong. He'd expected silence but this was a different sort of silence. He glanced into the nearest cage. Attila and three other pairs of eyes stared back. One behind the other, the four hens were straining against the bulging cage door.

Bill looked around. All the cage doors were bulging. Then he understood.

'Noooooooooooooooooo!' he screamed, desperately searching his pockets for a hammer and a piece of wire. Too late!

THWANG! The door of Attila's cage gave way.

THWANG! THWANG! THWANG! Doors burst open all over the battery house. Hens shot out like feathered rockets. Squarking! Flapping! Dust and pandemonium! Stunned by the flying door, Bill made a grab at Attila. She pecked him hard on his

fat nose as more hens joined the attack.

A huge cloud of hens, dust and feathers whirled out of the shed like a tornado. It bowled over the lumpy sons who'd been watching from the doorway. They fell against a stack of empty crates which toppled over just as poor battered Bill crawled out of the door holding his bleeding nose.

CRASH! The crates fell against the corner of the battery shed. It wasn't a very big crash but it was all the excuse the old shed needed. Very slowly at first, while the whole farm seemed to hold its breath, the wall that for years had told the world that Sunnycluck Farm was the home of happy hens, began to fall. 'Look out!' shouted Abel, and ran.

The rest of the hens had just enough time to escape through the gap, before the whole rotten structure crashed down on to the cages with a noise that would have gladdened the hearts of all the battery hens in the world.

The farmyard looked like a battlefield, with hens flying in all directions. They were everywhere, on roofs, up trees, being chased by dogs, pigs, the gang of men who'd come to help and the lorry driver. Bill was cursing under a pile of rotten wood and crates, and his sons were falling over each other trying to drag him out.

Attila kept her head. 'This way, sisters!' she said. After what they'd seen, the hens would have followed her right into the jaws of the soup monster.

'Charge!' she ordered and led them in a rush across the farmyard. They had to dodge sticks, flying boots and snapping teeth. But they didn't just run. The angry hens turned on their attackers.

It was a real battle and the old hen fought the hardest, scratching and pecking them back for a lifetime of unthinking cruelty. The lorry driver had soon had enough. He hid in his

lorry and nursed his wounds. 'Hens
don't do this,' he said.

Bill struggled to his feet. He wasn't
badly hurt and he wanted to get his
own back on Attila. He soon saw that
a large number of his hens were
about to get away.

'Quick! That big hen is leading them towards the gate!' he shouted. 'If they get in the corn we've lost 'em.'

Swinging his stick like a propellor, Bill was first to the gate. But before he could slam it shut, Attila and the leading hens were on him. He let out a roar and ran for his life as a great wave of hens poured through the gate, across the track and into the ripening corn.

Battery Bill's wife, Eva, watched from the kitchen window. She'd been wondering about all the noise and shouting from the yard. Bill suddenly appeared round the corner. He lunged at the farm gate, then disappeared in a cloud of angry hens, only to reappear, moving faster than he'd ever moved in his long, lazy life.

'Well, if that hasn't really made my day,' sighed Eva as she rocked to and fro with laughter. 'I never knew Bill could move so fast.' For years she'd begged Bill to give up battery hens, and now it looked as though the hens had got their own back. She wiped her eyes with the teacloth. 'Hens will be hens,' she said.

'And good luck to them.'

Later that night, Bill sat in the pub with a large plaster on his nose, staring into a pint of cider.

'I've never seen nothing like it,' he said. 'Twere like an 'orror film. This nasty great hen came straight at me followed by her whole horde, baying for my blood. 'Tis a wonder I'm alive to tell the tale.' He lifted his cider with a shaky hand. 'I always knew that hen would give me trouble, as sure as pigs is pigs.'

The round-up went on all day. Many of the hens never got out of the yard. They were soon caught and crammed into the crates. If the corn had been cut, the hens in the field would have been rounded up just as easily. As it was, many were hunted

down by the dogs. The rest had to
run, hide and run again. The hunters
continued the chase all through the
long hot hours until they gave up in
the falling darkness.

Attila watched from a small rise.
The ruin of the battery house looked
small and black as the sun sank
behind it. From different points in
the huge field she could see torches
wavering slowly through the corn as
the searchers trudged wearily
towards the lights of the farmhouse.
Still she didn't move. She heard the
distant rattle of crates being loaded,
one or two faint despairing cries.
Then the lorry engine roared, its

lights came on and slowly it
lumbered up the track to the road.
She watched until the two pinpoints
of red light merged into the
blackness of the plain. The soup lorry
had gone.

For a long time the big hen stared
sadly at the point where the lorry
had disappeared. The sound of the
engines faded. Silence had fallen on
the plain. Attila listened. She could
hear nothing but the whisper of a
breeze in the corn. How many of her
friends had survived the round-up?
Perhaps she was the only one left.
She shook herself and fluffed out her
feathers.

'No point in brooding. There's one way to find out.'

She stuck out her chest, took a huge breath, and stood right up on her toes and let out a squawk that echoed for miles across the plain and set the dogs barking in the farm below. Before the last echo had died away there were clucks and squawks from the corn in all directions.

For half an hour the hens called back and forth until Attila had a horde of about forty hens around her, clucking and gabbling about their escape, the battle at the farm and the long chase in the corn. Duster and Buster had made it and Attila could hear Paxo, as noisy as ever. She held up a wing for silence. 'Has anyone seen the old hen?'

No-one had seen her since the battle of the farmyard. This was a hard blow for Attila. She looked at the little band of hens and they looked back with complete trust, waiting for her orders. How could she lead them without the help of her friend? Well, she would just have to do the best she could.

'Sisters,' she began firmly. 'We must return to the farm.'

There were gasps and sobs and cries of 'Never!'

'Listen, we are surrounded by more food than we could ever eat, but we have no water. We need water before we can start our journey. We must drink from the farm pond.' The tired hens hung their heads. They thought about how thirsty they were. Attila was right.

Quietly the hens crept back towards the hated farm – closer and closer until they could see the two lumpy sons through the window, slumped on a huge sofa in front of the TV.

'Shuddup, you flea-bags, we can't hear a thing,' shouted Wayne and he threw the *TV Times* at the barking dogs. The horde was quite safe. A herd of hippos could have drunk the pond dry before Wayne and Abel moved from the comfortable chairs.

THE JOURNEY THROUGH THE CORN DESERT

They drank quickly from the slimy pond, then started their journey through the corn towards the last glow of the day. The stronger hens forced the way through the brittle stalks. About half a mile from the farm, Paxo, who was leading, tripped over a feathered bundle half hidden in the corn. It was the old hen. Her wing was broken and she was dying. Slowly she lifted her head.

'I knew you would come . . . I have waited to say goodbye.'

'Don't say that, we must take you with us,' said Attila desperately.

'No good . . . ' said the old hen.

' . . . Not in the dreams . . . I will die here . . . as sure as eggs is eggs . . . Goodbye, my friends . . . Goodbye and good cluck.' Her eyes closed and her head dropped on to her wing.

They all said goodbye as they filed past her but she never spoke again. Attila stayed quietly by her for as long as she dared, then whispered, 'Goodbye, old hen friend,' and hurried after the others.

The farm was still too close, so they moved on as quickly as they could. But they were exhausted. They were battery hens that had fought and run all through a day like no other. After half an hour the hens collapsed on a patch of flattened corn and huddled together beneath the stars for their first night of freedom.

Attila was woken by a sharp peck
in the side. Angrily she jumped up as
a large black crow flapped out of her
reach. 'Caw. Sorry, mate,' he
sniggered. 'I thought you was dead.'
The rest of the horde jumped up and
the crow took a few hops backwards.
'What are you hens doing out here
anyway? You should be tucked up
safely in your shed.'

'None of your business,' snapped
Attila.

'Cawse it is. Everything out here is our business, because there ain't nothing here but us crows and a fox or two.' The horde began to close around him. He hopped unhurriedly into the air. 'So you lot won't last long.' As he flapped away he called back at them: 'I shall be picking on your wishbones in no time at all.'

The hens stretched and flapped away the stiffness from the day before, pecked a little corn and set off, following their shadows away from the rising sun.

The crow was right about one thing – nothing seemed to live on the plain. They pushed on for mile after mile and saw nothing but dry earth and golden corn. It was hard going for birds that had spent all their lives cooped up in small cages. But this was their first real day of freedom. What were a few aches and pains compared with the joy of being in the great outside?

By the time they'd stopped and settled down for the second night, the joy was wearing a bit thin. There were mutterings and grumblings.

'When's she going to find us some water? I'm dry as a dust-bowl.'

'Why don't you ask her?'

'Not me! Duster, why don't you ask her?'

'Me!' said Duster. 'She'd peck my head off.'

Paxo flopped down beside them. 'What wouldn't I give for a nice long, cool drink of water,' she said, as loud as ever. The look she got from Attila shut them all up.

The next day was the same. Miles of tall, dry corn, aching legs, sore feet and dry throats. The crow was still following them and as the day wore on, more crows appeared. They hung high on the wind, watching and waiting as the line of hens crawled along the plain like a thin brown snake. As the snake crawled slower, the crows dropped lower.

A huge red sun was just touching
the top of the corn before Attila
allowed them to stop. By now the
hens were desperate with thirst.
They flopped on their backs with
their feet in the air, croaking.

'Water! Water!'

'We're done for!'

'Let the crows have what's left of
us.'

'I'd rather be in a can of soup. At
least it's wet.'

Attila was tired, thirsty and
worried. She blew her top. 'Get up,
you feather-brained, Kentucky Fried
leftovers. No-one dies here unless I
say so. We haven't come this far to
fatten black-hearted crows. You shall
get your water – soon.' She sounded
so mad and so sure that the hens
believed her, but they didn't get up.
They fell asleep right where they
were.

Why did I say that? thought Attila.

When the exhausted horde fell
asleep, the sky was clear and full of
stars. One by one the stars

disappeared as huge clouds rolled upwards over the plain. Deep rumbles carried on the still air didn't wake the tired birds, who slept on until a great crack split the sky. For a blink of time the whole plain froze blue-white. Then, in the blackness, huge drops of rain began hitting the corn around them. Splat! Splat! Splat! It fell faster, till the skies opened and it was like being inside a waterfall. The hens didn't know what to think. Could Attila really order a storm?

'Who cares?' said Duster. 'Let's drink!'

Frantically they drank the rain as it hissed and bubbled into the dry earth. They pecked at the drops running down the corn stalks until they could drink no more. As the sun rose, the sky cleared and the happy hens sat on the flattened corn and steamed.

Their luck had changed with the storm. They set off into a morning that flashed and sparkled in clear sunshine. There were puddles to drink from. Large patches of corn had been flattened by the rain and so the horde could move much faster.

The way led them gradually on to a high ridge. As they climbed the slope, the corn grew thicker. Attila led the way, forcing a path like a small bulldozer. She reached the top and suddenly there was no corn – only sky. There was grass beneath her feet, real green grass with flowers and things that hopped and buzzed. They had found one of the green roads that had been used by travellers on the plain for thousands of years. It rolled away westwards, like a long ribbon, following the ridge to the horizon.

For three days the horde travelled
the green road and, for the first time
in their lives, became real hens.
Everything green was tasted. They
scratched the earth for worms.
Anything that flew, buzzed or hopped
across their path had a dozen hens
chasing it. Bees, butterflies, daddy-
long-legs and dandelions. Sometimes
they caught and ate them.

Sometimes they wished they
hadn't.

Eventually the green road led them
to a small village, surrounded by a
fence that looked like rusty
brambles. The hens knew that
villages usually meant people, so
they approached very carefully.
Something was odd about the place.
Many of the houses had no roofs.
Brambles grew where gardens
should have been, and trees poked

through glassless windows. Next to the ruined church, standing on what had once been the village green, was a huge rusty machine. But there were no people. They had left a long time ago.

'It's Attila's dream!'

'Just as the old hen described it!'

'Hooray!' cheered the hens. 'We've found the land of grain and greenness.'

Attila felt uneasy. It didn't look much like her dream. 'I don't think we ought to stay here,' she said.

'But it is green and surrounded by grain,' said Buster. She desperately wanted to stay.

'Let's go and explore,' shouted Paxo, and off they all ran.

That seemed to settle it – they stayed.

HOME ON THE RANGE

The horde took over the village and settled down to an easy life of eating, squabbling and sitting about in the sun. Attila was thanked a thousand times for bringing them to such a wonderful place. She said nothing and went off to live on her own in the rusty old machine.

'What's she worrying about?' said Duster. 'This place is perfect. We've got everything we need and she mopes about as ratty as a rooster.'

Perched on the top of the old tank, Attila kept an eye on the village and the country beyond. Something was wrong. What had frightened away the people? What had made all the small round ponds? Was it those great red machines that crawled about the distant fields?

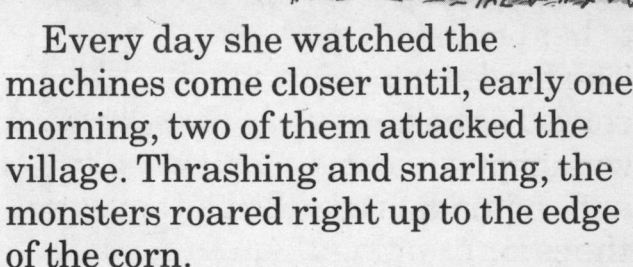

Every day she watched the machines come closer until, early one morning, two of them attacked the village. Thrashing and snarling, the monsters roared right up to the edge of the corn.

Round and round they went, belching smoke and spitting straw. Gobbling along behind them came a ravenous green scavenger. It grabbed the chewed straw, rolled it into huge round bales and dropped them all over the plain. The hens watched from their hiding places in fear and wonder. 'I think it's laying tractor eggs,' said Paxo.

Then the crow came back. He was perched about a mile away on a tall white pole with a red flag on it. Earlier in the day, Attila had seen a man in a jeep drive up to the pole, hoist the flag, and drive away. When the hens went to roost, the crow was still there. Attila didn't sleep well. At first light she flapped up to her perch to look for the crow. The pole was empty.

'Good riddance,' she said.

But the crow hadn't gone far. In a dead tree, close to the flagpole, sat a whole flock of crows. They were looking towards the village, waiting with the patience of vultures. When Attila warned the other hens they said, 'Who's afraid of a few tatty old crows?' and went off to look for breakfast.

It was a lovely morning with a cool breeze. Attila sat in the sun with one eye on the crows and one eye on Paxo. Paxo was still laying every day. She had a nest full of eggs in a bramble patch on the edge of the village green. All around, hens scratched happily in the sunshine. What could be more peaceful? Attila began to doze, only to be woken a little later by Paxo, squarking that she'd done it again. At the same time, from somewhere high above her head, came a long rushing whistle. There was a flash and a CRUMP! Paxo stopped mid-squawk in a woomph of smoke and flying earth. It looked as if Paxo had laid her last egg.

When the
smoke cleared,
Attila knew
where the
round ponds
had come from.
She watched a
cloud of feathers
drift slowly away
on the breeze. Poor old Paxo.

CLANG! The rusty old tank rang
like a bell hit by a huge hammer. The
big hen was blown high into the air,
did a triple somersault and was
running when she hit the ground.
She tore once around the village at
full speed, screaming at the terrified
hens, then away over the stubble like
a turkey with its tail on fire. The
horde went after her. They hadn't

heard a word of what she screamed at them over the bangs and crashes of exploding shells, but they understood that now might be a good time to leave.

About a mile from the village, the hens stopped running in the cover of some standing corn. The shelling had stopped. As the panting hens watched the smoke drift away, the flock of crows flapped lazily from their tree and glided towards the ruins. When Attila counted the horde they found that Maggie and Edwina were missing. But not Paxo – she was a few feathers short and as noisy as ever.

'All my lovely eggs,' she said. 'Smashed to little pieces.'

The shelling had shaken Attila as much as the rest of them, but she wasn't going to show it.

'We should never have stayed there,' she shouted. 'I told you but you wouldn't listen, so it's your fault.'

Before the shocked hens could argue, she pushed past them into the corn, heading once more towards the west.

HARVESTING AT SEA

Nobby Nelson had worked on farms since he'd left school at fourteen. He'd wanted to join the Navy but his mother wouldn't let him go. Nobby's favourite job on the farm was driving the combine-harvester. Some people thought it was boring, driving round and round the huge fields from dawn to dusk, but he loved it.

Perched in his cab high up on his harvester, he sang sea shanties at the top of his voice. As he ploughed his way across the waving sea of corn, he pretended he was the first mate on a tramp steamer, steering down to Shanghai through the South

China Sea. At the corners of the
fields he would shout things like,
'Aye, aye, Captain! Three points to
starboard and steady as she goes.'
Nobby kept a couple of bottles of
cider on board. He called it 'grog' and
said it helped him keep in tune. It
didn't.

All day the horde zigzagged
through the corn, trying to avoid the
harvesters. They'd first heard the
awful roaring engines soon after
they'd followed Attila that morning.

By moving away from the noise they had managed to keep out of danger, but down in the corn it wasn't easy to tell where the noise was coming from. At some time in the afternoon, tiredness made them careless and they got themselves right in front of two huge corn monsters. At first the hens tried to outrun them but they were much faster than they looked. Suddenly there was nowhere to go. The two monsters were right on top of them. Over the corn came the flailing paddles. Clackity! Clackity! Clackity! went the sharp teeth.

'It's going to eat us.'

'We're going to be scrunched.'

'Chopped and chewed and spat out in bits.'

'Over my dead body!' roared Attila. 'Sisters! Get behind me.'

They got behind her.

'CHAAARRRRRGE!'

They charged.

Nobby had had a good day. He'd finished his cider, and his imagination was in top gear.

'Eskimo swatting flying fish with a frying pan to port, Captain!' he shouted. 'Great white shark to starboard, eating sardines on toast!'

Towards the end of the second bottle of cider he had reported seeing an albatross with a sailor round its neck, following in their wake. So when he saw a horde of hens charging his vessel, it didn't seem much out of the ordinary.

'Horde of hens attacking dead ahead, Captain,' shouted Nobby.

Most of the horde were lucky. Their charge took them over the top of the corn. They were caught by the paddles, whirled around a couple of times and thrown back over the harvester.

Nobby watched the hens whizzing by, enjoying his daydream until a huge hen crashed through the windscreen, hit him in the chest and

landed in his lap like a dazed cannon-ball. This was real.

'Pirates!' screamed Nobby. 'Abandon ship!'

As he scrambled to get out of the cab, he knocked over an empty bottle and jammed the throttle open. Overboard went Nobby. Off went the harvester at full speed, across the stubble in a huge circle and back into the corn. Attila bounced about in the driving seat. She didn't know where she was, but wherever it was she didn't like it. Shakily, she hopped on to the steering wheel to try and jump out through the broken windscreen. The wheel moved under her weight. She hopped the other way, trying to get her balance. The machine seemed to get the idea. Here at last was a driver who really knew about harvesting.

With Attila staggering about on the wheel, the harvester roared through the corn in a perfect figure eight, looped a few loops and bounced off towards the other harvester.

The driver of the second machine hadn't seen Nobby dive overboard. He didn't realize anything was wrong until he saw the runaway coming straight at him, full speed ahead from the wrong side, being driven by a very large hen. He jumped off just before the two harvesters collided with a shattering crunch. Attila was thrown through the hole in the windscreen and landed with a bump next to the driver. They sat on the ground and gaped at each other in wonder for a moment, then ran off in opposite directions.

The harvesters were locked together like prehistoric monsters in mortal combat. Paddles thrashing, engines screaming, wheels spinning they tore into each other, digging up the earth and flattening the corn. The terrible teeth chewed into metal and rubber until black smoke turned into flame and the whole lot went up with a whoosh.

When Attila found the rest of the horde they were cheering like mad.

'Attila, Attila, the monster killer,' they chanted as they carried her off in triumph.

When the other driver found Nobby, he was doing the breaststroke in a pile of straw. 'Keep a weather eye out for sharks, shipmate,' he said.

ROAST CHICKEN

The fire from the burning harvesters quickly spread to the corn and soon the whole field was ablaze.

'Crumbs! What have we done?' said Duster, as the horde scuttled away across the stubble.

As night came on, a long line of flames licked all along the rim of the western skyline. The hens had never seen fire like this before and it frightened them.

'It looks as if we've set fire to the whole world,' said Buster.

It was a smaller and sadder horde that huddled together to sleep on the stubble. When Attila called their names she found that two more hens were missing. Sam and Ella had been eaten by the corn monster.

None of the hens slept well that night. A fine black ash drifted down from huge clouds of smoke that crept across the plain. Coughing and wheezing, they watched through red-rimmed eyes for the first signs of dawn. Eventually, a dirty yellow sun rose sluggishly through the haze, over fields that had turned from golden corn to black ash.

Attila looked towards the blackened horizon. 'That's the way we have to go.'

The horde didn't think that this was a good idea.

'We can't cross that, it'll poison us.'

'Look! It's still smoking.'

'We'll choke to death.'

'What if the fire comes back?'

For once the big hen didn't lose her temper. A bird that can destroy monsters two at a time shouldn't expect too much from ordinary hens.

'Well, we can't go back and we can't stay here,' she said in a snotty voice and marched off with her beak in the air. Reluctantly they followed her back to where smoke still rose from the blackened skeletons of the harvesters.

Crossing the burnt fields couldn't have been easier. The fine ash made them sneeze but it didn't scratch their legs like the stubble. Here and there the ground was still hot, making them hop sideways from one foot to the other like clowns running in big boots. They moved quickly, each step raising little black clouds of soot. Duster, trailing along behind as usual, had a bad sneezing fit. One of the hens looked round and sniggered.

'Hey! Look at Duster, she's even more dusty than usual.'

'Achooo . . . ! What about yourself, Sootface?' snapped Duster. 'You look

JUST LOOK AT YOU....

like you've been pulled through a . . .
Achoo! . . . chimney backwards.'

They all stopped and looked at
each other, then burst out cackling.
Attila didn't realize that she was as
filthy as the rest of them, and she
gave them all a dirty look.

'Just look at you. You're covered
from comb to claw. Now come on, we
haven't got all day.'

The ash ended suddenly when the
horde reached another field of
stubble where the straw had been
rolled into huge round bales. For a
while the hens scratched around for
grain left from harvesting, then they
settled down in the shade of one of
the bales.

Duster decided that this would be a
good time to ask the question that
had been worrying them all. She

didn't bother with small talk, she looked the big hen straight in the eye.

'What we want to know is, when did the old hen say we'd get there?'

'Yes,' said Buster. 'That is, if it wouldn't be too much trouble.'

'Yes,' piped the rest of the horde.

'When did the old hen say we'd reach the land of grain and greenness?'

Attila replied in the voice of someone who knows the answer but is not telling. 'Soon,' was all she said.

But 'soon' wasn't what Duster wanted to hear.

'Soon isn't good enough. We want to know *when* . . . ' she was hopping up and down, clouds of soot rising from her like a small volcano, ' . . . and we want to know now!'

Attila glared down at the scruffy little bird. Duster didn't care. Her squeaky little voice rose higher.

'And another thing. We're thirsty . . . and you're too bossy . . . and why . . ? '

Attila had turned bright red under the soot. Her eyes stood out like two small mushrooms in black compost. 'You snivelling little maggot,' she began. 'How dare you . . .'

'Ladies, ladies, calm yourselves, please.' A voice as smooth as silk came from somewhere above their heads and a big dog fox jumped down, as light as a cat, from his hiding place on top of the bale.

ARRAAAHH!! IT'S A DOG !!

'AAAAAHH! It's a dog!' screamed the horde, and they all tried to hide behind Attila at once.

The fox looked very hurt. 'A dog! A *dog* did you say? Me? A nasty smelly man-grovelling dog? Ladies! Ladies! How could you? I am a fox.' When he said the word 'fox' he made it sound like another word for all that was good and kind in the world. The horde relaxed a little, but he didn't fool Attila for a second.

'I don't care what you are. Clear off!'

'But, madam, surely you can't mean that?' purred the fox. 'Forgive me, but I overheard your lively discussion a few moments ago and I believe there is much I could do for you. I can lead you to the land you spoke of. Furthermore, I can show you where there is water. Why, just the other side of this very field bubbles a clear spring where you ladies may drink and . . . er . . . freshen up a little.'

Attila's eyes never left him. 'Get lost, we don't need your help.'

The fox looked as if he'd been poked in the eye by a Christmas fairy.

'I do assure you, madam, I have your very best interests at heart. If you should change your mind,' he smiled an oily smile at the other hens, 'just call. I shan't be far away.' Then he turned and loped off.

Attila wouldn't let them move for an hour. Carefully she looked all around the field before saying, 'This way!' and taking off in the direction of the fox's clear bubbling stream.

They found a muddy puddle that had been churned up by the combine-harvesters, but it was water and they drank it gratefully.

THE BUILDING OF THE PYRAMID

For the next few days the journey went well. It rained again and the hens had a great time flapping about until the soot was washed from their feathers. The horde had become more like wild birds. They were alert, bright-eyed and as fit as fleas. Combine-harvesters were everywhere, but they knew how to keep well away from them and they had learned to skirt around the fields upwind of the straw burning. The first ploughed fields puzzled them until, early one morning, a giant tractor, pulling a huge plough, appeared out of the mist as the horde were crossing a field of stubble. They watched from a safe distance.

'Why is it turning the earth inside out?' asked Buster.

'Perhaps it's looking for worms,' suggested Paxo.

No-one knew. There were no flocks of birds following the shining plough and the hens found little to peck at in the sour earth. The horde bobbed over the sharp furrows as quickly as they could.

For a while their luck held. The sun shone, the corn was high and the living was easy. Then, late in the afternoon, a hen called Hetty disappeared. The hens searched everywhere but found nothing but a few warm feathers on the stubble. At the same time the next day another hen disappeared. The horde became very jumpy.

Attila warned them to stay together. 'Above all, keep a lookout for the fox,' she said.

Duster had her own theory. 'Deserted,' she said. 'Done a runner. Couldn't stick being bossed about by you know who. Attila's made up the bit about the fox so's the rest of us don't run off.'

The frightened hens didn't know what to think. The fox's offer was tempting. On the other hand, they owed their lives to Attila. If only she would tell them more of her plans.

The big hen knew the horde were grumbling about her, but what could she tell them? Her only plan was to keep going westwards. So far, the old hen's words had come true. They'd had hardship and danger, surely it couldn't be far now. What the hens needed was some good news to cheer them up. I must find a high place, something I can climb to get a better view of what lies ahead, she thought.

In the next field of stubble they crossed, Attila found a straw bale on a slight rise. She flapped to the top. From there she could see that the plain sloped gradually upwards to the west, but the bale wasn't high enough. Jumping up and down didn't help much. Then she had an idea.

'Five large volunteers!' she shouted suddenly.

The horde had been watching her jumping up and down on the bale, muttering to herself.

'She's as dotty as the old hen,' said Duster.

'I think we ought to keep her happy,' said Buster.

Attila stood the five volunteers side by side on top of the bale.

'Four more!'

This lot were made to balance on the first five. They looked wobbly and worried.

'Three next! Come on! Come on!'

'She's mad!'

'Cracked as an egg!'

'Her brains have flown the coop.'

'Better do as she says – remember the corn monsters.'

The three managed to scramble up and now twelve hens swayed in the breeze on top of the bale.

'Right, two more on top.'

'No way!' said the horde. 'It's impossible.'

'No more! No more!' begged the bottom five hens.

Attila grabbed the last two 'volunteers'. Sheer fright got them to the top.

Now Attila began to climb. To a chorus of 'Ouch!' and 'Eeeck!' and 'Ahh! Me head!' she slowly flapped and clawed her way up the swaying, groaning pyramid. It was a real struggle for a big hen. Exhausted, she reached the top and stood teetering on the backs of the last two hens.

Now, whether it was an extra gust of wind, or whether it was the wisp of straw that the breeze dropped lightly on the end of Attila's beak, we shall never know. She had just enough time to glimpse an unbroken patchwork of gold and brown, rolling

up and away into the haze, before the whole feathery pile began to move. The bale was at the top of a slope and the weight of the hens, plus, perhaps, the last straw, started it trundling slowly downhill. For one glorious moment the pyramid held together while the bottom hens ran for their lives on the rolling bale. Then they crashed into a groaning heap on the stubble.

Attila sat amongst her bruised supporters. She was really disappointed that she hadn't got a glimpse of her dream but she was blowed if she was going to explain to the other hens.

'Well, I think that's enough PE for today,' she said in an offhand sort of way. 'Time to move on.'

They moved on. By now, most of the horde thought Attila was dotty, but they followed because they didn't know what else to do.

Harvesting hadn't yet begun on the higher parts of the plain. As the hens climbed upwards, the ridges of ripe corn stretched away above them, looking almost white in the distance, while below, the way they had come lay brown and dusty, like a beaten old doormat in the hot sun.

The next day was even hotter. Not a breath of wind stirred. Down in the dusty corn the ragged horde trudged along in silent misery, too parched to speak. The big hen nagged them to keep moving. She knew they wouldn't last another day without water.

The sun was still high when she allowed them to stop. They crouched in the corn, panting and praying for rain.

'Perhaps if we all close our eyes, cross our feathers and wish very hard, a nice little rain cloud will appear,' croaked Buster hopefully.

'Perhaps if we all cross our eyes and stand on our heads, Attila will ask the old hen for another thunderstorm,' said Duster sarcastically.

Without a word, Attila went for her. Duster, realizing that she'd gone too far, shot off, back down the way they had come. There was a screech. The whole horde jumped up to see what was wrong with the little hen. They found Duster unharmed, and the fox, smiling.

'My goodness me, ladies. Jogging? On a day like this? You should be sitting in the shade, sipping on something cool. As a matter of fact, I was just trotting along to a little pond I know. I would be delighted if any of you would care to join me.'

'Yes! Yes! We would! We would!' said all the horde at once, without waiting for Attila to speak. The big hen said nothing. She waited until the last hen had followed the fox back down the track and went after them. She was thirsty too.

The fox led them about half a mile to a dip in the plain, hidden by the corn. There was a small pond surrounded by rushes and low bushes, like an oasis in the desert.

When Attila reached the pond, the other hens ignored her. They sat in the shade of the bushes listening to the fox. 'Well, that's settled then, ladies,' he was saying. 'I shall return in the morning at first light. If you will allow yourselves to be guided by me, I shall find you somewhere that, in my humble opinion, is the perfect place for all hens to end their days.' He licked his lips and smiled at them all.

'Is this place very far from here?' asked Duster eagerly.

The fox gave an odd sort of snort, as if he was trying not to laugh. 'A lot nearer than you might think,' he said, waving his paw vaguely. 'A couple of days . . . maybe three. Now I must be running along.' He got up 'Till tomorrow then, ladies.' He bowed, then slid into the corn and vanished.

'He'll eat the lot of you,' said Attila. The horde turned on her.

'That's not true!'

'You're just jealous!'

'Because he knows where he's going and you don't.'

'Yes! And he saved our skins again today.'

Attila looked at them sadly. 'He's saving your skins for tomorrow,' she said and walked away to settle down at the other end of the pond.

That night, Attila slept with one eye open. She saw and heard nothing but there was one less when she counted the horde in the morning. The fox arrived, looking very pleased with himself.

'Rise and shine, ladies, your friendly guide is here.' Attila noticed a tiny feather sticking to his whiskers.

All through another long hot day, the fox led them across the plain. The hens mourned the loss of another friend but no-one spoke of it. In fact, they didn't talk much at all.

Early in the afternoon he stopped. The hens were tired but he seemed as fresh as ever.

'Ladies, I must leave you for a while. An urgent appointment. Keep straight on till I return.'

Later, when he found them again, he led them to a tiny spring at the base of a huge grey stone. It stood like the ghost of a giant, in a small grassy clearing. The horde had seen such stones before but always at a distance. They felt uneasy in its shadow. They felt more uneasy when the horde was counted. Clara was missing. She was a very popular hen. None of the frightened horde believed that she had run away.

'Got herself lost, I expect,' said the fox cheerfully. 'Oh well, must be on my way. Till cock crow tomorrow, ladies,' and he was gone.

The horde settled down nervously for the night at the edge of the clearing. Attila flapped to the top of the stone. As she closed her eyes she vowed to herself: 'I must do something soon before he eats the lot of us.'

The horde didn't sleep well. Attila slept better than she had done for days.

She woke
early when
the first rays
of the sun
caught the
top of the stone.
The ground was still in darkness but
she could just make out the shadow of
the sleeping horde. And there –
hidden in the corn – was another
shadow. Right, mister clever dick,
thought Attila. I'll give you a cock
crow you won't forget in a hurry.

'COCK-A-DOODLE-DOO!
WAKEY, WAKEY! RISE AND
SHINE!'

She launched herself from the top
of the stone, flapping and squawking,
right into the middle of the sleeping
horde. Terrified hens screeched in all
directions – and the shadow in the
corn vanished.

'It looked such a lovely morning I
thought I'd give you an early call,'
she cackled. The other birds gaped at
her in disbelief. When did Attila look
at lovely mornings?

'Nutty as a corncrake', said Duster.

Five minutes later the fox turned up looking sly and just a little ruffled. Attila's early call had made his hair stand on end.

'You're up very early,' he said, forgetting to smile and say 'ladies'.

'We thought we'd make an early start,' said Attila.

The fox ignored her.

'Well, if you're all ready, we'll be off . . . Come along.'

'What about my breakfast?' said Duster.

'We'll all be eating later on,' snapped the fox and he set off at a trot.

WE'LL CATCH A FOX

The fox hardly slowed down all day. Gradually the horde became strung out in a long line. Only Attila and the strongest hens managed to keep up. Again he stopped in the late afternoon with the same excuse. 'Business calls, ladies. Carry straight on and I'll catch up later.'

When he'd gone, Attila turned to the small group of hens behind her.

'Sisters,' she began. 'We have travelled a long way together. If you don't like the way I've led you, hard cluck! I've done my best. But you are my sisters. I care for you and look on you as friends. The fox is a fox and only looks on you as dinner. Give me a chance to prove that the fox is the enemy of all hens.'

Slowly, one by one, the hens agreed.

'Thank you,' said Attila, for the first time in her life.

DON'T WAIT FOR ME, WILL YOU ??.......

'Right! One of you stay here. As the stragglers catch up, show them which way we've gone. The rest of you follow me.'

Attila didn't carry straight on, she went after the fox. She was sure that he planned to double back, hide in the corn and grab the tail-ender. Sure enough, the trail led them in a big circle. He couldn't have been in any hurry. After ten minutes Attila whispered, 'There he is! I can just see the tip of his tail.' For about half a

mile they followed
the tail, keeping well back.
Suddenly it stopped, moved
forward slowly and stopped again.
'He's reached the edge of the trail,'
she murmured.

The little group edged closer. Time
passed. More hens joined them and
the story was whispered back from
bird to bird. Then they waited in the
hot, heavy silence.

The hens were staring so intently
at the white tip of the fox's tail, that
they all jumped at once when it
began to twitch.

'It's Duster,' said Attila, as they
heard Duster's squeaky little voice
come grumbling up the trail.

'Oh yes! This is nice, isn't it?
Don't wait for me, will you?
Oh no!' The tip of the tail
began lashing

from side to side. 'I could be torn to pieces by a Rhinostrich for all they care. I could be . . . Awk . . . !' The tail was gone. Frantically, all the hens rushed forward at once. They found the fox with Duster hanging limply from his jaws.

'Put her down,' said Attila calmly.

It was the big hen's lack of fear that had always bothered the fox. It wasn't natural. But then he thought: What's wrong with me? This is just a bunch of stupid battery hens. He dropped Duster on the ground.

'Well, ladies, so you've discovered my little secret. What a pity. Now I shall have to kill you all at once instead of one at a time.' The fox liked the sound of his own voice. There was no hurry.

'You know, you should never have left your nice, safe farm. Hens don't do that sort of thing. Your place in life is to sit around, sensibly laying eggs until it's time to be eaten.' He was enjoying his little speech.

'I'm not one to complain, but all this running around really does make you hens awfully tough. I mean, is it fair to those of us who have to eat you?' All the horde had caught up by now. The more the fox spoke, the angrier they got.

'Honestly, some of your sisters were hardly worth eating. As tough as old boots, in fact, and as for this scrawny little bag of bones . . . ' He prodded the dead Duster with his foot.

Duster had come to as soon as the fox had dropped her. His speech had fired her hot temper, but she'd decided it was safer to lie low. This last remark was too much. The 'scrawny little bag of bones' went for him. She was going to tear him limb from limb.

The fox was completely taken by surprise. He'd never been attacked by a dead chicken before. As he backed away, fending off the flaming Duster, the rest of the horde hit him. He quickly realized that this was no joke. These were large, tough hens fighting for their lives and they meant to hurt him. He turned on them, snapping and biting.

With a few quick snaps he killed two hens and injured some more, but they kept coming at him in a frenzy of pecking and scratching, snarling and screeching, feathers and fur. A claw raked his eye. His muzzle was a mass of pecks and gashes.

The fox was no hero – he ran.

When he was sure he had shaken them off, he turned and faced them. His cool manner had gone; this was a very different, dangerous animal. Ears back, he crouched low, with hackles up and one eye closed. His lips were drawn back in a snarl. Blood dripped from his muzzle on to the straw. He hissed, 'You haven't seen the last of me!' and was gone.

Attila stood in the middle of the flattened corn. Her battered horde lay all around her in the dust and feathers, too exhausted to move. The journey. The fight with the fox. The loss of so many friends had just about finished them. Eventually Duster got painfully to her feet and faced the big hen.

'We're sorry, Attila. We should have listened to you. What should we do now?'

Attila didn't know what to say. What could she tell them? They'd beaten the fox for the moment but as sure as night follows day, when he'd licked his wounds he'd be back to finish them off. Finally she said, 'The truth is that the old hen didn't ever tell me much more than she told you. All I've ever done was follow her plan towards the west and that's all we can do now. We must climb the ridge towards the setting sun. From the top we may see our future, one way or the other.'

This was the hardest part of all their journey. The stronger hens helped the weak and injured as they struggled upwards through the corn that seemed as thick as bamboo to the exhausted horde. The sun sank lower as they climbed the long shadow of the ridge. In her heart, Attila didn't have much hope left. In spite of her words to the other hens, she had all but given up her dream. I wonder if it will be the fox or the thirst that does for us in the end, she thought. Either way, the crows will be happy.

She could see them now, circling high above. Black rags in a soft pink sky.

THE CHICKENS COME
HOME TO ROOST

Within sight of the top of the ridge, the horde decided they could go no further.

'We've had it, Attila. We can't go another step.'

Attila was as beaten as they were but she couldn't stop. She forced herself on alone, until, beating at the corn with her wings, she collapsed in hopeless fury. The big hen closed her eyes. She thought bitterly of how unfair the world was. Why had they bothered to escape? The battery house was never this bad. They'd had plenty to eat and drink.

For a long time she lay in the dust.
She was just beginning to dream that
she was in her nice, safe cage when a
strange thing happened. Into her
head marched the old hen, Edwina,
Maggie, Clara and all her lost
friends. They began to shout rude
things at her.

'Get up, you great ugly lump.'
'Call yourself tough?'
'You couldn't beat an egg.'
'You couldn't crack a joke.'

Attila opened her eyes. She looked up at the ridge. Beyond the shadows the corn glowed red as if it stood at the very edge of a different world.

'I'll show you lot who's tough,' she said. Ignoring her pain and tiredness she got up and pushed her way through the last of the corn.

It took Attila a long time to convince the other hens that she wasn't raving. It took even longer to get them all to the top of the ridge, but it didn't matter, there was still enough light to see. They were standing at the top of huge grassy ramparts that dropped away hundreds of feet to a land of small fields, trees, hedges, little farms and fat cows. The edge of the plain stretched into the distance on either side like great green cliffs. Right at their feet, in a valley carved from the slope by a small stream, lay

Attila's dream: a crumbling
farmhouse set in a meadow. There
was the small wooden house, the
flowers, the orchard and the stream.
All that was missing were the hens.

It was Buster who broke the long
silence. 'Well,' she said quietly.
'What are we waiting for.'

The little wooden house looked
empty, but as the horde approached,
a head poked out of the door and
looked at them in surprise. Then a
large slightly gone-to-seed cockerel
strutted down the ramp towards
them. The hens hadn't seen anything
like him before. They thought he
must be some sort of over-the-top
chicken.

If he had known that these hens
had just seen off the very fox that had
taken his entire flock, only a month
before, he might have been more

careful. (He'd escaped because he'd dozed off on the roof at the time waiting to greet the dawn.)

'Good grief!' he squawked. 'Recruits, and about time too.' He strutted up and down, inspecting the silent hens. 'What a sorry-looking bunch,' he muttered.

'Obviously in need of care and protection. Where does HQ get them? Never mind! Soon get 'em knocked into shape. Fall in! Jump to it!'

Not a hen moved. 'Now look here,' spluttered the cockerel, growing redder. 'When I say jump, you . . .'

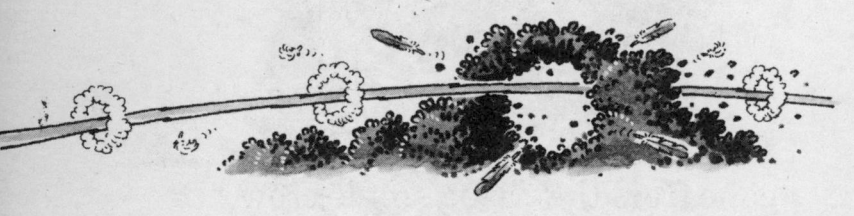

Hens don't do this, thought the cockerel on his third circuit of the hen house, with the horde hard at his heels. He cleared a hedge and kept running.

Attila was as close to being happy as she was ever likely to be. She was sitting in a straw-lined nesting box in the hen house. In front of her the horde roosted on long perches. So the old hen had been right. If only she could have been with them. She might have been able to help Attila with the one thing that still puzzled her. What about the chicks that she had seen in her dream? she thought.

Later, when most of the light had gone from the day, a single crow flapped high over the farm. His sharp eyes missed nothing. He could see a light in the farmhouse kitchen. He could just make out the cockerel, perched like a battered weather vane on the hen-house roof, while far away and above, on the very edge of the great plain, a one-eyed fox looked down.

THE END

ABOUT THE AUTHOR

PADDY MOUNTER left school at sixteen and spent five years at the Somerset College of Art, then ten years working in various design studios in London before moving back to Somerset as a freelance illustrator. Married with three children and a Jack Russell dog, his interests include singing and playing sax with an R & B band called The Flying Chapati Brothers. *Attila the Hen* is his first full-length children's book.

If you would like to receive a Newsletter about our new Children's books, just fill in the coupon below with your name and address (or copy it onto a separate piece of paper if you don't want to spoil your book) and send it to:

The Children's Books Editor
Transworld Publishers Ltd.
61–63 Uxbridge Road
Ealing
London W5 5SA

Please send me a Children's Newsletter:

Name: ....

Address: ....

....

....

All Children's Books are available at your bookshop or newsagent, or can be ordered from the following address:
Transworld Publishers Ltd.
Cash Sales Department,
P.O. Box 11, Falmouth, Cornwall TR10 9EN

Please send a cheque or postal order (no currency) and allow 80p for postage and packing for the first book plus 20p for each additional book ordered up to a maximum charge of £2.00 in UK.

B.F.P.O. customers please allow 80p for the first book and 20p for each additional book.

Overseas customers, including Eire, please allow £1.50 for postage and packing for the first book, £1.00 for the second book, and 30p for each subsequent title ordered.